Beauty and
the Pea

First published in 2013
by Wayland

Text copyright © Hilary Robinson 2013
Illustration copyright © Simona Sanfilippo 2013

Wayland
338 Euston Road
London NW1 3BH

Wayland Australia
Level 17/207 Kent Street
Sydney, NSW 2000

Series Editor: Louise John
Series design: Emil Dacanay
Design: Lisa Peacock
Consultant: Shirley Bickler

A CIP catalogue record for this book is available from the British Library.

ISBN 9780750268677
Printed in China

Wayland is a division of Hachette Children's Books,
an Hachette UK Company

www.hachette.co.uk

Beauty and the Pea

Written by Hilary Robinson
Illustrated by Simona Sanfilippo

WAYLAND

A shopkeeper called at Pea Castle,
and helped himself to a feast.
But little did he know that
Pea Castle was owned by a beast.

A wicked witch had cast a spell
on the beast, who was once a prince.

He'd hidden away in Pea Castle,
and been lonely ever since.

The witch had said that a kiss and a pea
would be the only magic powers,
that could turn the beast into a prince.
As well as a princess who liked flowers.

The shopkeeper slept at the castle
but, as he left, he plucked a red rose.

A booming voice said, "How dare you!"
The shopkeeper looked round and froze.

"You've slept and ate in my castle.
Now you've taken a rose from my door!"
"If you want to escape," said the beast.
"Tell me... who is the rose for?"

"For Beauty," the shopkeeper said, shaking.
"Your daughter?" asked the beast
with a wink.

"Here! Take all the red roses,
the yellow, the white and the pink!"

"Give her all these and then bring her to stay here with me for a while."

The shopkeeper said he would do so,
and the beast turned away with a smile.

Perhaps, he thought, she's a princess,
and the shopkeeper is really a king.

As the beast walked around his gardens,
his aching heart started to sing!

He made up her bed with a mattress,
after placing a pea on the base.

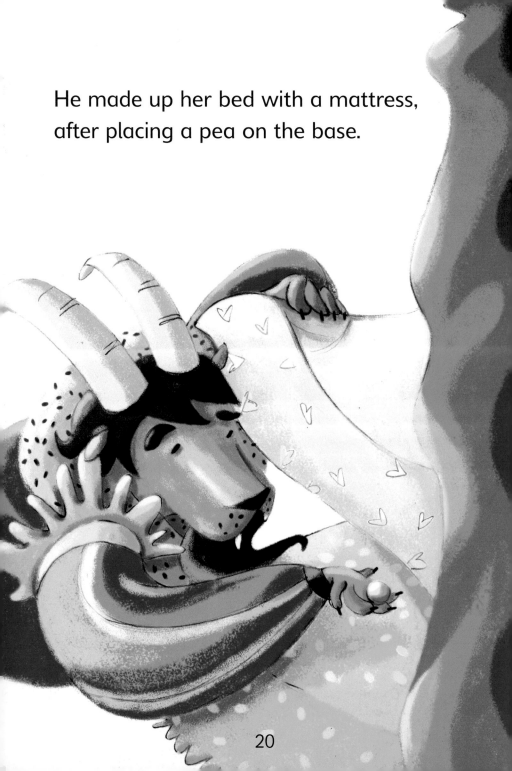

He laid a rose on her pillow,
and hung up curtains of lace.

Beauty stayed a week at Pea Castle,
to the beast's complete delight.

He asked if her mattress was comfy,
and if she'd slept through the night.

"I'm sorry I have not," said Beauty.
"There's such a big lump in my bed!"

Then beast knew she was not just a girl, but a beautiful princess instead.

He jumped up with joy and said, "Beauty!
I know I look ugly and smell,
but please kiss me once on my head,
to cast off a witch's mean spell."

Beauty did as he asked her,
and a prince appeared from the beast!

The very next day they were married...

... and served pea cake at the feast!

START READING is a series of highly enjoyable books for beginner readers. **The books have been carefully graded to match the Book Bands widely used in schools.** This enables readers to be sure they choose books that match their own reading ability.

Look out for the Band colour on the book in our Start Reading logo.

The Bands are:

Pink Band 1A & 1B

Red Band 2

Yellow Band 3

Blue Band 4

Green Band 5

Orange Band 6

Turquoise Band 7

Purple Band 8

Gold Band 9

START READING books can be read independently or shared with an adult. They promote the enjoyment of reading through satisfying stories, plays and non-fiction narratives, which are supporte.d by fun illustrations and photographs.

Hilary Robinson loves jumbling up stories and seeing how they turn out. Her life is a jumbled up lot of fun, too! Hilary writes books for children and produces radio programmes for BBC Radio 2 and, because she really likes doing both, she really feels as if she is living happily ever after!

Simona Sanfilippo loves to draw and paint all kinds of animals and people. She enjoyed reading illustrated fairytales as a child and hopes you will enjoy reading these fairytale jumbles, too!